G000068644

The Lynching Calendar

Jessica Starks

Published by Onion Publishing, 2019.

First Edition 2019

ISBN 978-1-7337647-0-4

Onion Publishing

P.O. Box 54

Pontotoc, MS 38863

This book is dedicated to victims, past and present, who never had a chance to fulfill their complete potential or tell their stories.

To my relative, L.Q. Ivy, who was lynched at seventeen years old. You will forever live in our hearts.

To my relatives who were forced to flee their homes in search of solace from racial terror.

For those who continue to suffer under the brutal hands of blatant injustice. This is for you. You are not forgotten.

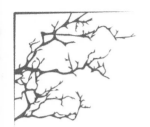

Prologue

Lynching is defined as "putting to death (as by hanging) by mob action without legal approval or permission" (Merriam Webster).

Notice that this definition does not mention anything about race; however, one can assume that upon reading the definition—or simply the word "lynching"—you associated the word with the turbulent history of race in America.

It's an unfortunate, however undeniable, reality.

Under the name of "justice," thousands of African and African-American people were brutally snatched from their families, friends, and communities. In the name of "order," entire black families were broken apart, and the psyches of later generations were forever cursed.

The word "lynching" is such a bitter word in the mouth of an African-American. It brings forth painful memories, sleepless nights, paranoia, and spiritual death. However, to progress with dignity and strength, one must remember those who did not have a chance to practice such resilience.

We must remember those who were jailed for learning how to read and write.

Beaten for forgetting to step off the sidewalk.

Tortured for loving someone of a different race.

Murdered for not saying, "Yes, sir."

We must remember those who felt cursed for being black.

Think of some of your loved ones—your mother, father, siblings, grandparents. Imagine the emotions that would dwell inside of you if you were given a box containing the last remnants of their being by someone who smirked at you as they gave you the tattered box.

1

Imagine how you would feel if one of their classmates or neighbors decided to accuse them of a horrendous crime that you, them, and God knows they never could commit, yet no one cares to hear you. The jury only needed one piece of evidence to convict them: a darker complexion.

One could go on and on and force the reader to continuously swallow these unsavory words, but what would be the purpose?

Rather than explain to you the savagery that occurred in centuries past, let's take a walk into the past and allow the voices to speak for themselves. The voices that never had a chance to speak. The voices that were eternally silenced through hate.

The voices that scream to be heard.

These are their stories.

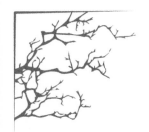

1
1954:
Ruby McNab

Youth is usually characterized as a thing of beauty: fledgling, yet strong and able bodies, wild and free without a care in the world. I used to believe this myself, until that hot summer day in 1954. That day, my entire existence changed in a single afternoon. In just a matter of hours, my innocence, along with my peace of mind, was stolen and replaced with the constant paranoia of reality returning to my doorstep, asking for a place to sleep.

Clarence James McNab, Jr. (CJ for short) was eleven years old when we met at the end of 1947. I was eleven too, but if you ever saw us together, you would probably think I was his daughter. I was 4'11" with a chest as flat as the ground, while he was 6'2" with the prettiest sable-colored skin. We were an odd pair, but we were the best of friends anyhow. Me and CJ did everything together: went to the movies, swam, picked sweet potatoes. Everything. We went through it all together, and we were inseparable because of it. That's why everyone was so surprised when I started courting his older brother, Willie.

Clarence loved the thought of me and Willie courting, and he always made sure his brother treated me right. My daddy left before I was born and my mama died having me, so I've always been my own family. Having CJ around gave me a sense of family that I'd never really had before. I finally had a big brother, someone who understood me.

Willie was a good man; he tried to spoil me every chance he got. Willie used to joke that he only did that in an effort to steal my heart from CJ.

Willie and me got married on December 20, 1952. That was the happiest day of our three lives. CJ's ultimate dream was to get married, so weddings always excited him. I wish I could have seen him get married. I always told CJ I'd find him a nice girl to settle down with, but he would just shrug me off, saying, "If God want me a wife, He'll tell me where to find her."

I was always jealous of his faith in God. CJ was one of the most God-fearing boys I knew. He had a Bible verse for every situation and a heart of pure gold. The Lord had big plans for him. While CJ was off doing the Lord's work, Willie and I began to focus on our family. The following year, I found myself getting ready to be a mother. The brothers were so excited that they both took on extra work in the fields to help save up. When Willie was at work, CJ and me were sitting at home listening to the radio, eating everything in sight. When CJ was at work, Willie ran out and got me everything I wanted to eat. Life was great! Everything was wonderful until Sasha Crawford came to town.

Sasha Crawford—what can I say about her? Sasha was simply the town's shame. Heck, she mighta been the state's shame for all I know. She was one of them "midnight women" and was always in and out of trouble. She always managed to get out of it though, 'cause she was a white woman. White women rarely get in trouble for anything around here. And on top of all that, she loved her some negro men. And when I say she loved them, she LOVED them. She was always prowling around the black sides of town looking for her next victim.

When word of Sasha's visit spread, every man in town stayed at home and didn't walk across their porches unless they had to. I was still pregnant at the time, so Willie and CJ were working like crazy in the fields. But they always made sure to go straight to work and come straight home. Usually, Sasha hung around the juke joints and other Godless places around town, so we figured the boys were safe, and they were... for a while.

One week, Willie had to go outta town for another job, so CJ was the only brother going to the fields. There just so happened to be a little abandoned house in the woods not too far from the field CJ worked in. It turned out that the little shack was Ms. Crawford's new home. Once CJ found out about it, he decided to stay home for a few days, but it was too late—the devil's plan had already been put into motion.

About a month went by and she was still there. CJ had to work, so he'd go back to that field occasionally, though he tried hard to get work elsewhere. He just couldn't find anything. He eventually had to break down and go back, but he tried to be watchful of her. Come March, I was into my fifth month, and CJ had already had a small run-in with Ms. Crawford, so he and Willie decided that it was best that he stay home 'til he could find work somewhere else. So, Willie would work and CJ would stay home and watch over me. CJ and I had so much fun during that time; CJ would buy me Cracklins and we'd sit around and read books, talk, and laugh all day. He'd even rub my feet if I asked; he was always spoiling me. I'm not even sure it had been a month later that word spread about Sasha Crawford's attack. Some white men were out hunting and found Sasha all bloody and bruised up. They say she said she had been raped and beaten. She was rushed to the white hospital across town. I heard that they had put her in this old, run-down hospital room since she was "a low-class version of white," but when she told them that she was raped by a Negro, they moved her to an even worse room than before.

Now, there's a couple things wrong with that, don't you think? First off: Sasha was the scum of the town, yet them white folks treated her with more respect than they ever would've a Negro woman. Second, they would've left a Negro woman in the woods to die. If the Negro woman was lucky, she'd be taken—not rushed, but casually taken —to another Negro's house to be tended to, probably 'til she died if it was bad enough.

It's possible. Not fair at all, but I guess life isn't always fair—especially for folks like us.

The week after, they called for all the men who worked in the fields to head on down to the police station, including Willie and CJ. Of course, I was worried, but I decided to do what CJ taught me: to put it in God's hands. Willie came back home after some hours, but we didn't hear nothing from CJ 'til the next morning—that's when we found out he was identified as Sasha's rapist. We were both distraught. We tried to go to the police station to get more information, but nobody would tell us anything. After days and days of trying, we were finally able to go see him in jail. I'll never forget the look on his face; his expression was something like a disturbed peace. I knew he was scared, but his faith in God allowed him to understand that no matter where he was taken or how he was taken there, his soul would always belong to God. He was content with that thought, so I knew we had no choice but to rest in it as well. A few days after our first visit with CJ, Sasha died from her injuries. That was when all hell broke loose.

The night she died, Willie and me went to see CJ. When we got there, he told us he already knew what had happened and that the sheriff told him that they'd be moving him to the next town over for his safety. I never spoke a word to Willie, but when CJ said those words an eerie feeling came over me. Somehow, I knew that I better relish in that moment with CJ; I wasn't so sure this chance would come again.

And that chance never did.

Never did any research of my own, but this is what I heard happened: Early the next morning, he was on his way outta town in a police car when an angry mob of white men attacked the car. The policeman who was driving tried to stop the mob, but they attacked him and kidnapped CJ. They dragged CJ to an old barn, where they interrogated and tortured him. That afternoon, they chained him to a wheelbarrow, put sticks and papers all around his body, and set him on fire. They said half the white folks in town were there, women and babies too. Some of 'em even made their own Negro workers come and watch. They said he suffered something serious. Of course, he did! He suffered not only from the flames but from the guilt of a crime he didn't commit! But he was strong; it took him two hours to die, they said. He was proclaiming his innocence to his last breath, I'm sure. My heart was crushed and my soul was broken. I was so shaken by it that I lost my baby. Willie never got over it either; every little thing reminded him of his brother.

There was no body to bury. All that was left was his heart, which was returned to us in an old shoebox. We wanted to move away and start over, but we couldn't afford it. So, we were forced to stay there, drowning in our own misery, each and every day.

Nobody talks about it anymore. Most everybody who lived through it done passed on or was too young to remember, so it's like it never even happened. Maybe it's better that way.

I sit and think about CJ from time to time—it hurts too much to think about it every day. I wonder what he would have been like now if he had a wife and family. That's something we'll never know. Because of what happened, I used to think he was the unlucky one, but then again maybe all of us who still live on this Earth are the ones who are truly unlucky. There's no doubt in my mind that CJ's in Heaven now, so he no longer has to suffer; he's happy and at peace. The rest of us are left to live our lives in this wicked and evil world. It's an endless cycle that I'd gladly be willing to exit whenever the Lord asks me; in death, I'll be reunited with my dear CJ again.

Sasha Crawford

Usually, when someone kills a man, they have the undeniable blood of their victim on their hands. It didn't exactly work out that way for me, though. Perhaps it's because I didn't kill him physically; plenty of men have his blood on their hands for that. Doesn't make me any more innocent, though. It might just make me more guilty.

I was well-known as the scum of the Earth around the town, and I can't say I deny it. I did a lot of things that weren't very ladylike back then. CJ changed my life, though. Guess I changed his too, huh?

I was born not too far from where he was lynched, in a little ol' run-down farmhouse. My mama was a seamstress, and my daddy was a share-cropper. I had a twin brother, Jared, who was six minutes my elder. We didn't have much money, so we were looked down upon just as all the Negroes. Don't get me wrong; we were still superior—we made sure they respected us. My mama almost shot a Negro girl for telling Jared his eyes were pretty. That's just how life was, nobody really knew why.

As I got older, I began to want what any girl my age dreamed of: a boy to like me. Since we couldn't mix much with higher-class whites and none of the lower-class ones were to my liking, I decided to make do with what I had: Negro boys. I didn't realize how easy it would be to catch the attention of a Negro boy; I didn't think they cared too much about any white girl 'cause of the fear. But I think they loved the taboo just as much as I loved the attention.

It was a well-kept secret 'til I got my first boyfriend. Marvin Depriest was his name; he was one of the darkest Negroes I had ever met in my life—real smart though. One day we met behind my daddy's shed while my parents went to town. He seemed happy, but I was annoyed. Don't

8

get me wrong, I liked the attention, but the romance was too easy; I couldn't stand it. But I carried on with it anyway. We sat and talked for a while, 'til I decided to be bold and kiss him on the cheek. Right when it happened, my brother popped up out of the house and saw the whole thing. Marvin ran off and Jared told my daddy the whole thing when he and mama got home. Mama was so angry and upset. She called me a "Nigger-loving whore" and told me she couldn't bear to look at me. My daddy wound up escorting me out—my clothes in one hand, his shotgun in another.

Poor white folks are basically Negroes, so most people refused to help me out. So I went to the Negroes, who I grew to love even more than before. Guess you could say that's where the legend was born. By the time I was sixteen, everybody, especially the Negroes, knew my name. I was always at the local juke joints, trying to find my next meal; I always found it too. I'll admit, though, there was always something inside of me, telling me, "Sasha, this ain't the life for you." But I had to survive—I couldn't go back home, so I had no choice in the matter.

Around the beginning of 1953, I came into CJ's town. A boyfriend I had at the time had given me some money and an old, rundown little house he had off in the woods. It wasn't much, but at least I could say I had somewhere stable to lay my head at night. Never really had any visitors, since everyone in town avoided me like the plague—that's why I was surprised Clarence was so nice to me. Wish more people in the world were like he was.

It was kinda funny how we crossed paths, though. I loved living out by the fields 'cause there was an endless supply of Negro boys. I caught a couple of them, but the one I really wanted was Clarence. He was what I always wanted: a challenge. I never did catch him though. It seemed more like he got me instead.

I was chopping some wood one day—or at least trying to. He was in the field working when he saw me. I could tell he hesitated when he realized who I was, but he decided to help anyway. I, being the infamous

Sasha Crawford, was determined to show him why I was so famous. I started giving him compliments and laughing at his jokes. All men love that. It strokes their ego, you know? I thought I might have had him, so I decided to use the kicker: "You're the most handsome Negro I have ever seen in my life!" I'll never forget what he said: "Well, I am made in God's image. Thanks though," he laughed. Then he flashed me an oddly innocent smile and kept on chopping. That usually got them every time, so I was both confused and mad. Then he asked, "Excuse me, ma'am, I don't mean to pry... but do you know Jesus?" I just looked at the ground and shook my head. "No. People have tried to tell me about him, but no." When he left, he promised he'd be back with a Bible for me to look at.

That night I laid in bed trying to figure out why he didn't take the bait. I knew if I wanted to get him, it would take a little more work.

The next day he was back like he said he'd be, Bible and all. I put on the nicest dress I had and made sure I looked real pretty—enough for a Negro, anyway. It was all in vain, though; all I got was learning about God. I must admit, though... I did feel different after the conversation.

Days, maybe weeks, went by and I never heard from Clarence. I can't lie, I was angry about it. I never even saw him in the fields, which worried me. But my anger overtook my concern. That's why I decided to frame him.

I killed a stray cat and captured all the blood I could. Then I pinched myself a few times. I bruise easy, so it wasn't hard to make it look like I had been beaten up. After that, I just laid down in the yard around the time I knew the men would be in the woods, and I waited. They eventually found me and the whole act was a success. The hospital was alright. Since I was a "nigger-lover", I knew they wouldn't dare check me, so I just relaxed and let my testimony to the police do all the work. Despite my reputation as a dirty and loose woman, they treated me nice and believed everything I said. I could have told them Clarence said the sky was green and they still would have believed me and charged him with something. Funny, ain't it? The next few days they took every nigger man that worked in those fields and brought them together for a lineup; that boy Clarence was one of them. Soon as he walked up, I pegged him and gave the best performance of my life. I cried and screamed and fainted, made them believe I was reliving the rape. They arrested him right on the spot. I was satisfied; I got my revenge. But that night, my past and my conscience came after me.

The nurse told me I had a visitor. I never had any visitors, since no one in town liked me, so I figured it was one of my male suitors. To my surprise, though, it was my twin brother Jared. I hadn't been home in over ten years, but I would see Jared around from time to time. He refused to speak to me in public, but when no one else was around he would slip me some money or tell me how Mama and Daddy were doing. Outside of that, we had no connection to each other. When he came, I thought he was coming to check on me because he cared, but that wasn't the case. Instead, he said, "Sasha Ruth Crawford! How could you do something like this to yourself?! You know better than to keep messing around with those nigger boys! Gah, I bet you didn't even get raped. I sure hope you ain't pregnant! You'll rot in hell for the hell you've caused—both to the nigger you arrested and to this family!" He had no sympathy of any kind! It almost made me cry, but I'd been told worse.

But then I got to thinking about Clarence. He was probably miserable; maybe I really would rot in hell. It'd be better than the one I was living in, though. After a few tears and a lot more thinking, I decided to fill myself with a whole bottle of pain medicine. I came into this world unloved, and that's the exactly the way I left it.

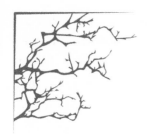

CJ McNab

The Bible says, "God does great things which we cannot comprehend." It also says that our lives are but a vapor. I learned these lessons in their totality during the summer of 1954. I was born right at the end of 1936, literally. I was born seconds between 1936 and 1937, which caused the midwives to argue over my birthday. So, I would just celebrate the last day of December or the first day of January—whichever one I felt like.

God called my parents home when I was six years old and my brother Willie Bernard was ten. I remember that day like no other: the house fire. We still ain't sure what started it, but my father immediately rose to whisk the family to safety. Willie said he smelled the smoke but thought he was dreaming. We both woke up to Daddy yelling, "Fire! Get out of the house!"

As we was trying to get out, we heard Daddy talking to Mama, "Come on, Viola. I'll carry you out." My mama had not been able to walk since I was born and needed help getting around. Mama said, "Don't worry about me, get the boys." My daddy rushed to get us out and the last glimpse of my mama was her struggling to get outta bed and choking on smoke.

My daddy put us on the front lawn and told us to stay there as he went back in to get Mama. We lived out in the country with the next house about fifteen miles away, so we had no one to come for us while we waited for Daddy to come back. We waited and waited and waited. He never did come out of the house. My brother later told me Daddy had asthma, which is probably why they didn't make it out. Everything in the house was destroyed. We literally had nothing left but each other and the clothes on our backs. When the fire subsided, we recovered what was left of our parents' bodies and buried them by a nearby old oak tree that had been damaged by lightning a few years earlier. Me and Willie would go by and visit their graves every so often. As we went on, Willie and I established our own life; we got jobs at a local farm and met some nice folks who let us rent out their house. A couple years later, I met my best friend, Ruby. We were eleven when we met, but I could have sworn she was only about seven — she was so little! But she never did let her smallness fool you. She was a feisty one! She could be the sweetest thing, but if you ever made her mad she'd set you straight!

But I loved her; she meant the world to me. She felt like my little sister. She was my little sister. That's one of the reasons I was happy she married Willie Bernard; she would be a member of our family forever.

They had a real nice wedding. I'll be honest, I was a bit jealous because I had always wanted to be married, but at the same time I kind of knew I never would. Negro girls didn't take to me much, not sure why. White girls would stare as I walked by, but I didn't want to get into that kind of trouble. Ain't that some irony...

Right at the beginning of summer, Sasha Crawford came to town. Whenever she came through, all the Negro men knew to hide. Some feared it would ruin their reputation, some feared they would lose their jobs, some even feared temptation; she was just that lethal. I don't really know why I hid, 'cause I wasn't that afraid of her. Guess I just hopped on the bandwagon.

I remember the first time I met her. I was working in the fields, and she was outside her house chopping wood. At first, I didn't recognize her; I just saw a white woman in the country struggling to chop wood. She was still struggling to chop wood by the time I got off, so I went over to help her out. As I got closer and closer, I realized that it was Sasha Crawford. I was shocked and nervous, but not necessarily scared. She had already spotted me, so I had to keep going anyway. I was kind of shy, so I nervously approached her to offer my services; she seemed more than happy to accept my offer. White girls, good or bad, are all the same. They all laugh the same, use the same sly remarks, and all flirt the same. She was trying her hardest to get me; it was funny. I just kept reminding her that I belonged to God and no one else. As we chatted and I chopped wood, I decided to ask her if she knew Jesus. Her confused look, along with her saying "No" made me happy. I loved the idea of saving a soul, and I planned to set my sights on saving Sasha's.

The next day I returned to her with my Bible. I told her about how God sent Jesus to rid us of sin and the life she was living wasn't God's plan for her. The longer we talked, the more intrigued she looked, and her happiness showed me that my work wasn't in vain. I prayed with her and then left.

Somebody saw me leaving the woods and told my brother. I told him I helped Sasha with some wood, and he made me stay home for a while. It was probably about two weeks, not too long. But not long after that, word spread that Sasha had been found beaten in her front yard and she said she had been raped. None of us believed it. I mean, no disrespect to her, but who would rape a woman who offered herself freely to men?

Nonetheless, the police had all the men from the fields go to the hospital so they could see if one of us was the rapist. Sure enough, she looked dead at me and said, "Him. That's the one right there!" Then she went into a screaming and crying fit and had the nerve to wink and grin at me! Everyone was shocked. They all knew it wasn't me, but really, what chance did a bunch of Negroes have against white cops? I just kept reciting the Lord's Prayer to keep myself calm.

They immediately locked me up. They wouldn't let me see my family, but knowing Ruby and Willie Bernard, they'd fight it. After what felt like an eternity, they did exactly what I said and came to see me. It was bittersweet, though, because I never wanted Ruby to see me that way and my brother, who was always protecting me, felt completely helpless. I knew God was gonna take care of me, but I felt so angry! I was freeing Miss Crawford from bondage, but she betrayed me! It really tested my faith.

How could someone be so cruel? But I just prayed and asked God to help me forgive her.

I was so distraught that hours, days, and weeks didn't matter anymore. I was told that, two weeks after I had been in jail, Sasha had passed away. Ruby told me that it was rumored that she had never really been raped, so I'm not sure what she died of. I thought maybe she had been robbed and beaten, so perhaps she died of the injuries she suffered. Even though I was still bitter, I prayed to God for her soul, and for mine as well. That was all I could really do at that point.

I can still remember it; right after I finished praying, they unlocked my cell and put me in the back of a police car. A sense of urgency came over me, but I tried to stay as calm as possible. Nothing good can come of a negro man in the care of a white man at night. Everything was peaceful until a big group of white men started walking towards our moving car. At first it just looked like two or three of them walking by on the left side of the road. But then I noticed about four more to the right start following the car as we passed by. Of course I was nervous, but I knew I was in trouble when the officer started looking around.

Next thing I know, something hit the back window of the car. I turned around to discover at least three more men following behind the police car! I knew then that I wasn't gonna reach my next destination.

They stormed the car, attacked the policeman driving, and grabbed me up. Next thing I remember, I was being dragged to an old barn and was hogtied.

They spit on me, called me all kinds of ungodly names, and beat me. They told me to confess that I killed Sasha, but I denied it. I was innocent. There was no reason for me to lie; I'd lose either way. I might as well lose with a clear conscience.

They punched me in the stomach and kicked me in the head. They ripped my clothes off and did ungodly things to me. They kept asking me to admit my guilt, but I wouldn't budge. At one point one of the men said they'd let me go if I accepted guilt. Desperate, I claimed guilt. But they lied! They continued to torture me! They grabbed my naked body and defiled me in the most intimate ways no human being should ever have to experience. I'm sure my screams of agony could be heard all over town that day. By the time they were finished with me, I could barely keep my eyes open. They were so bloody and swollen I kept them shut. I could feel the blood and bile between my legs coagulate. The last thing I remember hearing was people chanting, "Kill that nigger! Kill that nigger!" At that moment, I think I was the one who wished for death the most.

My head injuries were so severe that I could feel my torturers grab me by my then-broken shoulders and drag me. The wisps of clay dirt that were kicked up by the dozens of shoes walking around irritated my many scrapes and gashes.

I remember being strapped to something, though I couldn't make out what it was. I could see shadows of movement, but I couldn't hear or comprehend.

The first thing that hit me was the smell. It was musky. It was metallic. Rank. Stale. The stench brought back memories of the fire my parents were in. The sensation of the fire against my clothes brought me back to reality. I was being burned alive.

I was completely numb. I knew what was happening to me, but I couldn't fight it, no matter how hard I tried. They stood around me, laughing and cheering as my body burned. They stood there and watched me die, and nobody shed a tear. I kept screaming out, "I didn't do it! I'm innocent!", but it was no use. They wanted justice. They wanted to make an example out of me.

I eventually stopped trying. My skin was burning, melting, searing. It was no use. I accepted my fate. Taking one last look into the distance, I saw an old tree that looked like it had been struck by lightning. My mother and father emerged from behind the tree. The look in their eyes told me, "It's time to come home."

And home I went.

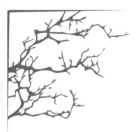

Willie McNab

What's a man to do without a family of his own? Almost everyone close to me is gone. With CJ gone, Ruby's all I got left.

CJ and I was four years apart, but you couldn't tell. My baby brother always seemed older than he was. It sometimes got on my nerves, 'cause he would try to tell me what to do. But most times he was telling me right. I never let him know that, though. Our mama and daddy died when we was young, so we was all each other had, you know? No aunts or uncles or nothing were here to take care of us, so we took care of ourselves. I loved my baby brother, not only because of who he was but because of the example he was for me and for bringing me Ru. When I first met Ru, I could have sworn she was a child—she was so little! Still is to this day. But don't let her short self fool you - she's got a lot of heart. One of the reasons I married her. When CJ first died, Ru tried to talk to me about it, help me feel better, you know. But it was too much for me to handle. I just couldn't face it. One week me and him was walking to work together, talking like we always do, then Sasha comes into town, and we're called to talk to the police, and then... he's gone.

My baby brother was gone.

Being the oldest, you always think you gonna go first. When the tables are turned, it's a pain you can't imagine. I'm not much for talking, but when it all happened... I sometimes worry that not talking about it is what made Ru lose the baby. It was a boy. We were gonna name him Titus. It was a strong name, so he'd grow up to a be a strong man. I hate that his daddy wasn't strong enough for him.

Ruby and I never had kids after that. She couldn't have no more, no matter how hard we tried. Maybe it was for the best. Neither one of us could stand another loss.

I've come to make my peace with CJ's death, I think Ruby has too. He's gone, I just gotta keep going. Folks still whisper here and there about it, but I try to pay it no mind. I got tired of living under the shadow of fear a long time ago—CJ wouldn't want me to live that way.

CJ taught me the *Bible*. He's the reason I'm the Christian man I am today. I miss him a lot, but I know he's way better off than us.

Sometimes I'll go for walks and go back to where him and Mama and Daddy are. It's like I can still feel him there. I sit and talk to them for a while. They help me feel better about everything. I'm an old man now, and I know my time is winding down. I'm ready to go. I miss my family. I want to see them again. Me and Ru will finally get to be with Titus again. No more worry, pain, bills, racist white folk.

I know CJ made it. I hope to make it too.

Like I said, I don't say too much, but I loved my brother, I love my wife, and I love the good Lord. That's all that matters.

2
1911:
Mallie & Malcus Finch

"My name's Mallie."

"And my name is Malcus."

"My son and I were both lynched on August 21, 1911. I was fifty-six and he was nineteen."

"Guess you could blame me for it," sighed Malcus.

"Malcus, don't—"

"Mama, it's alright. I was accused of stealing a cow from somebody's farm. Maybe I could have saved us if I hadn't fought back." "You tried to prove your innocence and defend your home, ain't nothing ever wrong with that," said Mallie. "Ain't nothing wrong with that.."

"Yeah, I know, mama. I didn't mean to—"

"Wait, Malcus. Let's just start from the beginning."

"All right," said Malcus. "Well, we lived in a fairly big town in the West. My daddy died when I was young, and I was my mama's only child, so I became the man of the house early. I couldn't do much. I mostly did little odd jobs around town to provide for myself, Mama, and Ma Phera. I cut grass, fetched groceries, stuff like that. Always got food on the table somehow," Malcus said.

"Yeah, it was hard for him to find a job 'cause he was a young black man," Mallie mentioned. "But it was hard for all of us to find work sometimes, 'cause we didn't go to church. We didn't believe in all the God stuff—we believed our ancestors guided and protected us, not some strange deity that nobody can see. They kicked my baby out of the colored school because of it. They told us that since we couldn't welcome Jesus into our hearts, they couldn't welcome us into their school. My mama became his learnin' after that. She was a good teacher too.

She taught him literature, herbs, spells—everything he needed. Shoot, I even learned some new stuff myself! Our family came from a long line of bushmen, so it was only natural that Malcus be one too. Even his father descended from Indian medicine men on one side of his family."

"It was in my blood. My fate. What I was created to do. People were afraid of us, so most times we had to keep to ourselves and do everything in secret. That's how we got in trouble," Malcus continued. For some of our spells we needed animal blood in order for them to work. And for this particular spell, I needed the blood of a heifer. All we had were bulls, so I tried to save up to buy us a female cow. After about three months of saving, I had enough to buy a small heifer from Mr. Rainswell down the street. I gave him the money and told him I'd be back later to come get my cow with my mama. Our family had known Mr. Rainswell for years and we had bought cows and chickens from him before, so this exchange was no different. When we went back to get the heifer, Mr. Rainswell wasn't at home. So Mama spoke to Mrs. Rainswell and told her about the deal. Mrs. Rainswell was always a prude woman. And I was afraid she'd be scared of me, so I had mama talk to her instead."

"Yeah, ha!" Millie interrupted. "Went and talked to that woman about the cow and she looked at me like she had seen a ghost! It's like she thought I was gonna hurt her. I was bein' polite though. But I know how white folks are, especially white women. They're so prim and proper and can't stand us old black witches for nothing. But in all truth, shouldn't we be just as scared of them as they are of us? Anyway, we got the cow and headed back home and, as is custom, we let the cow fatten up some and then kill it, that way we'll have plenty of blood and meat to use."

"The cow was fine," Malcus began, "not hurt or nothin'. But that same night, a group of men came to the house. They had fire in their hands and stormed in the house. They grabbed Mama, so I shot and injured a man's leg. That got 'em real mad then."

"Yea. They couldn't see, since it was so dark, so I grabbed the gun from Malcus and ran. I hoped that they would chase me and spare my son."

"I ran too," began Malcus. "I was ahead of 'em pretty good, but one of their dogs caught me. I'll never forget the pain I felt when that dog's teeth sank into my leg. It's so degrading to be hunted down like a rabbit and to lie on the ground captured, surrounded by bloodthirsty demons just itching to take your life from you. Not long after that, they caught Mama too. She shot the dog trying to get away, but it was too late. And her shot killed the dog, which just made them devils madder. They dragged us, kicking and screaming, to an old barn some miles from our house. That night into the next morning they beat us. They beat us so bad. They took my belt off and choked me with it while making me watch Mama get pistol whipped. They tried to make us say we stole the cow, but we didn't budge. Then I started hearing voices. Tons of voices were screaming and spitting at me. 'You stupid niggers can't keep your hands to yourself, neither will we!' they said. 'We hate all you niggers!' 'Dumb blackies!' I silently recited a tranquility chant Ma Phera taught me to calm myself. Then everything went black. All I could hear was evil laughter, but I didn't know where it came from. I was so delirious from being beaten half to death that I couldn't figure it out."

"Something similar happened to me," Mallie interjected. "I couldn't really see much either, they had beaten me in the head so badly. I tried to keep my head up high, to show that they couldn't break my spirit. I also did that because I felt like if I would have looked down my eye might have rolled out of its socket and onto the ground. The three voices talked to me as Malcus and I were led to the bridge. They sounded similar to the ones that beat us, yet this time they weren't calling us 'stupid' or 'nigger', they were reciting Bible scriptures.

Then I finally understood what was going on. I knew I was going to die. I knew my son was too. "In the middle of my trance, I was jerked back to reality with a push. For a split second, I felt myself floating in mid-air. Suddenly my body was numb. I knew the time had come."

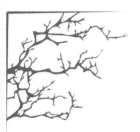

Phera Finch

I n my long life and many experiences, I've come to learn that there isn't a spell or remedy for everything. And nothing will ever be able to cure a broken heart.

I didn't even know anything was wrong 'til I woke up in the middle of the night to a house full of commotion. I was confined to a wheelchair, so I couldn't maneuver like my daughter and grandbaby could. I fell out of bed trying to get into my wheelchair and hurt my hip so bad that I couldn't move. Suddenly, I heard a gunshot. It was my cue to stay quiet, so I didn't even try to call out for help or move. The pain from my hip was so intense that it knocked me out, so I didn't come to until the next morning.

When I woke up, I immediately knew something was wrong—I could feel it in the air. I said a chant for strength and managed to scoot over to my bedroom door and pull it open. My heart just sank when I looked into the kitchen; tables and chairs were flipped over, papers scattered, bullet casings—the room was a mess. No sign of Mallie or Malcus at all. And the house was silent. The kind of deafening silence that makes you uneasy.

The kind of silence that can make you lose your mind.

The kind of silence that screams out loneliness.

I was beyond worried.

I thought Mallie and Malcus would be back before long. They never did return. I couldn't make it without them. I'm a feeble old woman; how can I protect myself? A neighbor found me and got me cleaned up, but I knew I wouldn't last long on my own.

Two mornings later the postman came to deliver mail to my house. We usually never got mail, so I wasn't sure what to expect. That morning, a single postcard, addressed to me, came. No message or nothing, just a postcard. I didn't think anything of it at first until I looked at the picture. Postcards with lynched negroes were fairly commonplace, but this one was different; it was Mallie and Malcus! My babies! I just dropped the card and sobbed. I sobbed until I couldn't breathe anymore. I was supposed to go first, not them! Surprisingly, I made it three years after their deaths. I died surrounded by nothingness. We didn't have any other family; I lived alone. I spent my last moments engulfed in the silence that replaced the presence that was Mallie and Malcus.

I died peacefully at ninety-two years old, going in my sleep. Sadly, my babies never got that chance.

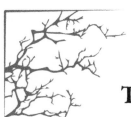

Thomas Rainswell

M y wife is stupid. She's just ignorant. I always knew she would go too far one of these days. And she finally did it.

I've been doing business with the Finch family for a long time. My family was poor, so we all worked in the fields together. Mister Finch, Phera's husband, was always an honorable man. They had some strange ways, but Mister was always fair and level-headed. He never learned how to read, but that man couldn't be cheated out of no money, that's for sure. In any other situation, I wouldn't live next door to no niggers, but I was fine with them. They were really some decent folks.

When Cynthia and I got married, we decided to stay in the family home and make a life here. We have two boys and a girl of our own. They all went off and married and started lives of their own, except for my oldest boy; he wants to be a playboy, travel the world and do art. I think it's a waste of time, but Cynthia would fuss me to death if she heard me say that.

Anyway, Malcus came to me every so often to do business. He usually bought eggs or milk from me. Malcus looked a lot like his grandfather but he had his daddy's personality. I didn't know his daddy much before he died, but he wasn't one to hold his tongue, black or white. But he was a fair man too.

Anyway, They'd bought cows and pigs from me before, but I normally handled it all myself. Cynthia didn't really deal with them much. She always claimed to feel uncomfortable and sick whenever they came around. I would play like I heard her and understood, but I didn't care. He had money and fairness like his grandaddy and that was enough for me. Long as his money was green, I didn't care about the color of his skin when it came to business dealings and makin' some extra money.

That particular time, the boy told me he had something to do so he'd be back the next day to get the cow—no big deal. I forgot I was heading to a funeral the next morning, so I just told Cynthia that they'd gotten a cow and to be there in case they showed up. But leave it to her to make a big deal out of nothing.

When I got home, she was hysterical, climbing all on me, telling me what happened. Then she tells me that she got the sheriff out here for a report. Sheriff Williams was a joke! He was a fat dupe of a man who almost never did his job. Plus, I think Cynthia was so afraid of Mallie that she didn't know what to do with herself.

I'll be honest, I was shocked when I saw the postcard. I guess the sheriff actually did something for once.

Cynthia Rainswell

I didn't know what those niggers was doing. I was afraid for my life. I did what I thought was right and what would keep me safe. I've known the Finch family for a number of years. My daddy used to own them; my maiden name is Finch. Phera was my wet nurse when I was a child. I respected Phera for that, but I never have liked that daughter of hers.

Mallie Finch has always been unladylike. She drank all the time, was always making spells, and was just the strangest nigger girl I had ever met in my life. I never did understand how she and Phera shared the same blood; I used to tell my girlfriends that all the time. They were just as frightened of her as I was. Thomas, my husband, told me that they might be by, but I didn't know what for. He never tells me anything. So when they came gallivanting up to my front porch talking some nonsense about a cow, I just froze. It was almost as if I was entranced, that's what I told my girlfriends. I had never been that close to Mallie Finch before. She was hideous! Her features were fair for a nigger, I guess, but it was her skin that bothered me. It was so dark, I couldn't bear it! It was terrible, poor girl. Her mother was a darkie too, but it was just different. And when she walked away... Mallie had always been thin, but she had such a large bottom and hips. She was just a disaster. Calvin, Malcus' father, was always handsome for a nigger. I always thought he too good for her.

When they started taking the cow I panicked and I called the sheriff, who came out as quick as he could and got my story. I always have liked our sheriff. Such a kind and gentle man.

When Thomas came home, I told him what happened. I told him about how they scared me so but, as usual, he ignored me. He's so incon-

27

siderate. He pushed me away and explained to me that they had bought a cow and came to pick it up. When I told him that I called the sheriff, he just laughed and said, "Our sheriff is lazy. He don't care nothing about two niggers and a cow!"

He stopped laughing when he saw the postcard. Our sheriff does do his job, no matter what Thomas says.

Do I feel guilty? Course not! For what? I didn't kill anybody, I'm not a murderer. I did my civic duty and reported what I thought was a crime. My hands are perfectly clean.

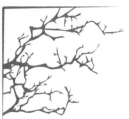

3
1865:
Renée Brushard

I guess you could consider my life to be something like that story, Romeo and Juliet: so beautiful, yet a tragic love story in the end.

Just when something begins to feel right, reality comes back to haunt you.

I lived in Lamont, Louisiana at the end of the Civil War. My family had been in Louisiana since they were purchased and brought here from South Carolina, so naturally it has always been home to us. There were still some kinds of slavery, but negroes were starting to have more freedoms in our little town. Some negroes had homes and businesses, some married wealthy, some even mixed and started families with the local French—I was one of those individuals. Of course, there was still those who wanted slavery to continue and spread hatred, but everything was safe, or so I thought. I was a maid on the Brushard Plantation, located in the heart of Lamont. Legally I was still considered property, since I was a young negro girl, but they never treated me as such; I was treated like one of their children. They let me go to school and get a job, make a life for myself. Life was great. I remember sometimes wishing that I'd been born white so I could keep this life and have it become even more amazing.

Claude Arnett came into my life when I was sixteen years old. His family had also been lifelong citizens of Lamont and were heavily involved in the community. They owned a lot of land, their family was involved in the government, and they had lots of money and power. Though only two years my junior, he had the heart and soul of a man twice his age. I was headed from visiting a friend, and he was just taking a stroll down the road, I guess. We were passing each other, and he stopped to talk to me. I'm more of the shy type, but he was as friendly as ever. We talked for a minute, and then we went on our way. I thought we would split ways, but he kept walking and talking to me. In the end, he wound up walking me all the way home. It wasn't a long walk, but by the time it was over he had made a major impression on me. He was smart, quick-witted, and extremely funny. He was also handsome; he had eyes blue as the sky, and his dark brown hair just whipped effortlessly in the breeze. He was just a lovely creation all around.

Claude continued to come to see me after our first meeting. We would spend hours just talking and looking up at the clouds; I loved those days. I was young and gradually falling in love. It was perfect.

I didn't realize how serious his feelings were until my eighteenth birthday. I was asleep in my bed when I was awoken by taps on my window. I assumed it was some troublesome kids terrorizing the neighborhood again, so I slowly walked up to the window with a switch I kept for them in the corner. However, I was surprised to find Claude. "Whoa, what are you doing with that?" laughed Claude when he saw my hand raised with the switch, ready to reprimand some children. "I'm sorry, I thought you were some of the Margeux children. They like to come wreak havoc at night sometimes. What are you doing here so late anyway?" I asked before kissing his pale cheek. I made sure to put my switch away.

"I came to give you your birthday present! Come on!" I wasn't exactly sure why he had to sneak me away from the plantation, but I didn't care—I just loved being with Claude. He had amazing energy. It was addictive.

Claude and I wound up stopping near a little country store that his family owned, not too far from where I lived. We snuck inside and he gave me some candy. "Is this my gift?" I asked, slightly disappointed.

"No, no. Hang on." Claude went to the back of the store and returned with a small box. "Here's the real gift." Inside the box was a small gold locket with a four-leaf clover inside. "Claude... this is beautiful! This is for me?"

"Yes, all for you, *ma belle*."

He told me that as long as I kept that locket, we would always be together. I remember looking at him all wide-eyed, saying, "You really mean it, Claude?"

"Of course, I mean it. Why, Renée Brushard, I do believe I love you just that much." He gave me the sweetest kiss on the cheek. Who knew three words could mean so much.

By my twentieth birthday, things with our relationship had changed slightly. Claude still made my heart skip a beat, but sometimes I wondered if I did the same for him. There'd been rumors going around town that he'd been messin' around with other negro girls and denying his acquaintance with me in public when I wasn't around. Every time I'd try to talk to him about it, he'd get angry and tell me to stop listening to such nonsense. He never said if the "nonsense" was true or not. But I loved him, so I tried to make the best of things anyway.

My family tried to tell me, "Renée, be careful. Just 'cause a man say he love you don't mean he really do. Claude is sneaky, he's only trying to get one thing out of you, and when he do he's gonna be gone." I listened and understood what they were tryna tell me, but in my heart I honestly felt that Claude wasn't like that; he was a good man. And they were wrong about him only wanting one thing and leaving. He didn't leave—he was always by my side. He always came back to me. If no one else loved me, I knew Claude did. And he proved it throughout my entire pregnancy.

When I told him about the baby, he had the most perplexed look on his face. He said, "With me?"

"Of course, silly! Who else would it be?"

"I don't know... just asking. Okay, umm... okay."

"Aren't you excited?"

"Uhh... yeah. I'm excited, *ma belle*," he said as he gave me a hug. I could tell he was nervous, but I knew we'd be just fine.

Claude immediately sprung into action. He bought me new clothes, went shopping for me, everything. He told me he didn't want me to step out of the house or off the plantation unless absolutely necessary.

Since I was still legally Brushard property, he couldn't move me away without permission from the family, so every time anyone came to see me, he told them I was sick or out. He said he wanted to protect me from getting sick from other folks. He took good care of me. My family and friends on the plantation thought it was strange, but I knew he meant well. I understood their frustration, but I think they were too hard on him sometimes.

When I hit six months, I was huge! Clothes could no longer hide my belly and Claude's protection over me could no longer hide his infidelity. One day while Claude was gone, I snuck out into the woods to take a walk and get some fresh air. I hadn't been out by myself in almost two months, so it felt good to experience new scenery. Tired, I plopped down on an old log and took a rest. I always did enjoy just taking in the scenery. Sometimes Claude and I would sneak into the woods and talk and laugh. I found myself thinking about how we would soon be able to take the baby with us to the spot.

Suddenly, I heard leaves rustling and giggles in the distance. Next thing I know, I see a petite, young mulatto girl running toward me. Alarmed, she stopped. I immediately laughed and asked her to help me up. She did, and we talked for a second. We eventually got on the subject of why she was running. She told me she was hiding from a boy she was seeing... his name was Claude.

"Oh...Claude who, if you don't mind me asking," I inquired. The girl, whose name was River, responded, "Arnett. His family is really rich. He's so handsome! Claude Arnett... don't his name just make you wanna melt?!"

This news caused me to cut the rest of the conversation short and head back home. "See you around! And congratulations on your baby!" I muttered the best 'thank you' I could, but I rushed back home with tears streaming down my face.

Claude came home later that night with leaves in his hair and a red mark on his neck.

Garrett Henry Brushard was born the August of my twenty-first year. Garrett was a beautiful baby. He came out with smooth, chestnut skin and dark blue eyes just like his father. I hate Claude missed the birth, he would've been so proud. He wasn't home when I went into labor, so one of the local midwives, unaware I was even pregnant, delivered my precious baby. I was in love. He was the perfect little baby.

Claude came to see me about a week later. I asked where he had been, but he just ignored me. He went over to Garrett, picked him up, and said, "This is the child?" When I nodded, he walked back out the door with the baby in his arms. I chased after him and asked what he was doing. He said, "We're gonna take a walk." I tried to go with him, but he kept insisting that I stay in the house. I was still in some pain, but something inside told me to grab my baby, so I snatched him up and ran back in the house. Claude ran after me and kicked the door in so I ran out the back and into the woods. Claude chased after me for a while, but soon gave up the chase. My baby spent the second week of his life hiding in the woods with his mama.

But we eventually had to go back home. I needed food because I ran out of milk for my baby. When I got back home, I expected to find Claude there, but instead I was greeted by an older French woman, whom I had never seen before. As soon as she saw me, she eerily scanned me and the baby up and down and said, "Well hello, dear. It's about time you came back home."

"Who are you?" I gripped my baby even tighter.

"I'm Annette, Claude's mother. He told me about what happened... about the baby."

"Oh, you're here to meet your grandson! This is him right here!" as I moved Garrett's blanket to show her his precious face.

"Grandson. Hmm. I'm here to fetch the child so we can all forget that this... mishap ever happened. Give me the child, dear," she said as she reached for my baby. I jerked away and a slight tussle ensued. I ran away again, back into the woods. As Annette left, panting and frustrated, she yelled out, "It's your decision! You'll pay for what you've done to my family!" I had no idea as to what she meant, but I didn't have time to think about it—I had to take care of my baby. By the next morning, me and Garrett were on the run again. Claude never came back home, so I left a note with one of the fellow slaves to give to him that explained what had happened, in case he came looking for me. It pained me to leave him, but I had to protect my child—our child.

Garrett and I hid in plain sight in the next town for a month and a half. As Garrett got older, he looked more and more like his father; it was almost uncanny. We'd be walking down the street and folks would stop us and say, "My, my! That baby is precious!" Anytime someone claimed that he looked like one of the Arnetts, I would just laugh it off and change the subject. I couldn't afford for anyone to catch on. It's not that I was ashamed of Claude. I loved him. I just knew that I couldn't draw attention to our family. I wanted things to work out between Claude and I, I truly did. But I was slowly learning to accept life as a single mother.

Around Garrett's sixth month, Claude showed up on my doorstep. He told me he missed our family and wanted to make sure we got what we deserved. I was overjoyed; I knew he'd come back for us! I wasn't sure how he found us, but I was sure glad he did. I had made a whole new life for myself and Garrett, but our family just wasn't complete without Claude. Now it finally was.

My joy was cut short a week later when a group of white men burst into our home, grabbed me up, and dragged me outside. I screamed for Claude, but he couldn't move, two men were holding him back too. Thank God I kissed Garrett and told him how much I loved him earlier that day because I knew I wouldn't see him again. At least he would have his father.

The men took me into the woods behind my house. As they slapped and spit on me, they told me that they weren't about to let someone like me shame the Arnett family name. Suddenly emerged my sweetheart, Claude, but there was suddenly something different about him. Claude looked at the men and told them to back away and leave us to ourselves. I was confused, but I was happy he came back for me. I instantly told him I loved him and asked him where Garrett was, but he just started telling me not to worry, that he was sorry for everything that had happened and embraced me with the warmest, fullest hug he had ever given me before. As I listened to my love's heartbeat, I felt a sudden sharp pain in my side.

Then another.

Then another.

I looked at Claude. I was speechless. Before I could even think to say anything, he kissed me on my forehead and walked away. I tried to call out to him as my body fell to the ground, but I couldn't. My heart slowly broke into a million pieces as my vision faded and I watched him leave my side.

I was so naive. How could I have been so blind? Claude Arnett never loved me and never will. Why couldn't he have just left me alone? I left town, he could have just forgotten about me. He stripped Garrett of a loving mother. For that, he will never be forgiven.

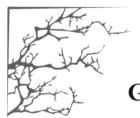

Garrett Brushard

How would you feel if everyone in town knew you were the mulatto baby whose mother was murdered by his father? I don't really remember my mother. I have one old picture of her not too long before she died and a little gold locket with a four-leaf clover that was around her neck when she died to remember her by. One of my uncles gave it to me when I was little to remember my mother. He told me he used to come visit me and my mama when I was a baby and he's the one who found me alone in the house and my mama dead in the back. There's still a little bit of her blood stained the inside. One thing I'll never forget is her voice and her scent. Everyone who remembers my mother said she couldn't sing a lick, but I remember it differently; her voice was so calm and soothing—not perfect, but just right for me. As for her scent, I distinctly remember being cradled in large whips of lavender. Still love lavender to this day.

I was six months old when I became an orphan. Thank God for the Brushard family; they came and got me right away, once they learned of my mother's tragic death. Apparently, my father tried to put up a fight and keep me, but legally I was owned by the Brushards.

Therefore, my life was spared. I just know he would have killed me if I would have stayed under his care.

In some ways, I miss my mother, but at the same time I'm glad she's gone. Don't get me wrong, I wish my Mama could have raised me and loved me and took care of me, but at least she is with the Lord now. She doesn't have to suffer because of her skin color and her love for my father anymore. She can be happy and free, where she is surrounded by people who love her just as much as I would have.

Haven't laid eyes on my father since I was taken away from him. Doesn't really bother me. Madam Brushard always says, "The Lord says honor your mother and father. They gave you life." But Claude Arnett can burn in hell for all I care. How can I honor someone who did what he did to my mother? I just don't understand how someone can be so cruel! My mama loved him with all her heart, and he killed her! That's not how I was taught to show my affection for someone. I'm eighteen now. My mama would be proud of me, I hope. I still look like my father, which gets me a lot of attention, but I don't abuse it like he did. The Brushards got me in one of the best negro schools in Louisiana. They always tell me how much my mama wanted for me and how they promised to do the best they could to keep her dreams for me going. Sometimes when I'm alone or when I'm worried or upset, I'll hear a sweet voice singing in the distance, or the scent of lavender will flutter across my nostrils. That's when I know that Mama is with me and that everything is gonna be just fine.

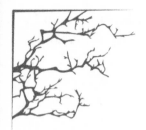

Claude Arnett

If there's one thing I've learned in age, it's that life goes on. I was raised in a somewhat racist family. My family was full of people who claimed to hate everything about Negroes, yet behind closed doors, it was a totally different story. Both my mama and my daddy had at least one affair with a negro man or woman. I'm sure there were more, though. So, of course their blood runs through my veins—I like Negro women too.

Renée... Brushard? I haven't heard that name in a long time. I don't remember where, when, or how she and I met, but I do remember that she was something special when I saw her. Those full lips and that pear shape... What man in his right mind, negro or white, would pass that up?

I was young when we met, maybe fifteen or sixteen. I was young, handsome, hot, and ready to go. She caught my attention, so I ran with it.

Was Renée the only one? No, no. I courted plenty of negro and white women at the same time, and I enjoyed every minute of it. Sometimes I felt bad for being unfaithful, but she knew about it. If she didn't like it, she could have easily left. But she didn't. I enjoyed doing what I wanted with her, and that was all that mattered to me. When she got pregnant, it wasn't a big deal. Plenty of girls had gotten pregnant by me. I had already had two fully white children she didn't know about and a half-black baby girl on the way when she told me the news. Only thing is, she let it spill to everyone that the baby was mine! When the other negro girl got pregnant, she knew better than to tell the world that I was the father, but Renée was young and really naive. She stayed cooped up on the Brushard place and never really lived life. Quite sad, really.

But anyway, she ruined my reputation when she started telling. Some of my girls stopped seeing me, upset that I was having a child with someone else, angry that I slept with both races, or worried that they might be next. It was terrible. And not only that, but my parents heard rumors about it and I had to tell the truth. Mama had plenty of pregnancies that she never carried full term because she didn't want our name tarnished. They told me to ask for her to kill the baby, but I knew she wouldn't do it. I knew I had to do something, though.

I didn't know how far along she was and was trying to keep my other girls happy, so I didn't go see her for a long while. I had originally planned to just beat her up pretty bad and make her lose it, but she had already had the baby when I finally decided to go back to see her! I got drunk because I hit harder when I've been drinking, so seeing the baby there just made me even angrier. If I'd had it my way, and the law hadn't gotten involved, the boy wouldn't be around either.

But I'm old now. The boy's probably an adult by now, or somewhere near it. No use in trying to deny him. They say he looks just like me, but a negro, you know? Says he's real smart too. People talk about how nice and caring he is. He's got his mama's spirit, that's what that is.

Never married. No kids that claim me. I have a few friends here, but most of them moved off. So, I'm just an old lonely man. As much as I'd like to disagree, some whisper that I deserve to be alone, that I deserve every bad thing I get. I don't know, maybe I do. But, even if I cared to, I can't change the past. Life keeps going, whether you want it to or not.

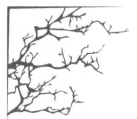

4
1948:
Julius Johnston

N ame's Julius. Julius Johnston. I was born in the winter of 1867 in Paducah, Kentucky. I died two days before I would celebrate my eighty-first birthday in 1948.

A little about me: my first wife, Lydia, passed having my only son Jefferson. I needed help raising Jefferson so I married again. She died from a sickness ten years later. Figured I better stop marrying or every negro woman in Kentucky would be dead!

I raised Jefferson mostly by myself. I thought that raising a man-child would be fairly easy, since I'm a man myself, but it was rough. I loved my son, but it was always something about him; he couldn't be trusted. Thought it'd get better as he got older, but instead it got much worse. As a teenager, he started getting mixed up with the wrong crowd and became a gambler. Broke my heart; I never wanted that for him. I worked and worked all those years so he could have a good life, not a tarnished name.

Jefferson never married, at least not to my knowledge. Wouldn't expect him to. Jefferson was never really the marrying type. He couldn't really keep a steady job so he couldn't provide, and he was always busy always trying to seek approval and acceptance, like he was a child. Any woman that would even think to marry Jefferson would be an absolute fool.

I'll admit, Jeff did improve a little bit by the time he got into his twenties. He was at home more, helped me out; he was the son I needed him to be. Something still didn't feel right though, and I was always on guard.

The night before I was killed, something told me to just sit with Jefferson and tell him I loved him. So that's what I did. I spent the day with him, and we just talked, told stories, cracked jokes, and shared secrets. We did what every father and son should do. That was a great day for me, and hopefully for him too.

Later that night, Jefferson told me he was going to meet some friends and that he'd be back later. I wanted to believe him, but I know my son. He was up to something with the worst people possible. Around eleven o'clock, I heard a stout knock on the door. I figured it was my boy, since nobody else comes to the house that late. However, it wasn't my boy on the other side of the door.

A young lady, no older than my son, stood at the door smiling at me. She told me she was trying to get to her sister's house but couldn't seem to find the street she lived on. I found it odd that a young pretty girl such as her would be out alone this late at night, but I chose to help her anyway. I tried to explain where the street would be, but she told me she had a bad memory and asked if I could write the directions down for her. Obliging, I invited her in to sit while I wrote the directions down. As I went to grab a pencil and some paper, I asked the young lady her name, to which she replied "Callie". I began some small talk about where she was from and who her sister was, but our conversation was cut short by a group of men suddenly bursting through my door and into my house. I'm an old man, so my reflexes weren't like they used to be. I was shocked; I didn't know what to do or think. The men tackled me, told me not to say nothing, and covered my head with an old sack and tied my hands behind my back. I could tell they took me outside because I could feel the callousness of the cold night air and the gravel between my toes. Suddenly I could feel the men putting something around my wrists. When they put my hands down, all I could hear was the rocks cracking under boots and then a door slam. At the same time, I heard the car engine rev up, I remember being swept off my feet and kissing the fresh sediment. I suffered like that for almost thirty minutes, which felt like an eternity to me. When it ended, my body was badly burned and my hip and wrists were broken. Terrible way to leave this world, but at least it was me and not my son.

Jefferson Johnston

Name's Jefferson Johnston. Julius was my father. Did he get killed? Yes. Am I the reason why? Well... yes, but I never meant to have him hurt, and especially not killed! Swear to God I didn't! My pops was a good man... he just happened to have a nobody for a son.

Life was hard sometimes, but I always knew I had my pops. He busted his butt trying to give me a good life, and he did. He really did. No, he may not have been the most affectionate man, but he's a man—what can you expect? My real mom died having me and my stepmom died when I was young, so we didn't have the softness of a woman in the house. But I always knew he was trying and he showed me love the best way he knew how. I loved my pops, I really did.

I was a shy kid and didn't have friends, so when I finally got me some I wanted to keep them, no matter the cost. That's how I got into gambling.

At first, I didn't know I was much of a gambler. They told me I was a natural at it though, so I thought it was okay. It started with simple stuff like betting on dog fights and boxing matches; then it went to craps and poker. I was never really good at much and nobody really cared about what I did, but this was something I could do and got attention for. People accepted me! I didn't want to lose that!

They needed me just as much as I needed them.

Every bet I made ended in my favor—I was like a savior to those people. I was on top of the world—well, my world. I kept all my doings from pops. I knew he wouldn't approve and would try to talk me out of it. He knew I wasn't much good. I didn't want to stop though; I wanted money, friends, women, happiness—a real life. Then after I'd saved enough,

I'd handle my pops. I planned to build him a new house, buy him a car. I knew he would have been proud of me then.

Then I met Callie. She was the most beautiful girl I'd ever seen in my life! Wow! I couldn't have her though; she was the girlfriend of one of the most powerful gamblers in the town, and one of my main competitors. He'd been trying to get over on me for years but never could. He didn't like that too much. I always thought Callie was too pretty and sweet to be with Jorge. She was smart too. Because of him, she was given a good education, better than anything she could have gotten in Mexico, where she was from. Maybe that's why she stayed with him—he gave her a good life. Can't blame her.

I remember when I first met Callie. She had on this pale pink dress that stopped just under the knee. Her hair was in a long braid down her back, which initially made me think she was a teenager, but the way she carried herself made her seem like a mature woman. I was sitting in the lounge of this old gambler's club when she and Jorge came in. I was just laid back, but when she looked my way with those beautiful eyes, my back straightened up. Almost as if she demanded nothing but excellence when she came in. I loved it.

Jorge had her sit down across from me in the lounge. We just looked at each other for a minute. "How are you?"

"Fine, thank you. How are you?" Callie said as she smirked down at the floor.

"I'm good."

"That's good." Callie looked away. I was worried she was losing interest in the conversation until she quickly glanced back at me. I did my best to keep the conversation going.

"You... with Jorge?"

"Yeah."

"Okay." I looked around the room nervously, as if I were expecting someone to slap me in the face with something else to talk to her about, but it never came. I never was that smooth with the ladies. It was super awkward at first, but then "Open the Door Richard" came on. My dad never understood why I loved that record so much, but it just always brought my spirits up somehow. I think everyone has a song like that. It just makes you smile. Just like Callie did. Ha, I remember mouthing the words to myself and all of a sudden I hear her whisper, "Open the door, Richard" along with the music. When she noticed I caught her sheepishly singing along, we shared a laugh.

That's how our friendship started.

I had it bad for Callie, though. And it didn't take long, either. I had it so bad that I decided to sell my soul to the devil. I had just gotten in good with Jorge and started working for him, which meant I got more chances to see and speak to Callie. We had great conversations and she taught me a lot. I really started falling hard for her then, and I think she began to feel the same way. My love for Callie eventually started getting in the way of my gambling and I started losing bets. It was terrible, my whole world began to turn upside down. But that was just the beginning. One day I was sitting at Jorge's house waiting to head out for a dogfight. When I asked if he was ready to head out, he told me that Callie decided she wanted to go and was getting ready. After a brief pause, he looked me in the eye with a big grin and said, "If I ever catch you and Callie together... if you even look at her or think about her... I'm gonna get you where it hurts. And you know I ain't lying."

Scared me out of my wits, but I had to suck it up quick because Callie showed up right after that. I knew what Jorge was capable of. His fellas used to pick on me and a couple other fellas I knew when we used to play against each other. I heard he even shot a man in front of his family—wife and kids. That's cold, but that was Jorge. And I didn't want no part of it. I didn't look at Callie the whole night, much less talk to her.

After the dogfight, I stayed home with Pops, the one person I knew wouldn't be taken away from me. We spent the next day together, just enjoying each other's company. Nothing special at all, we just sat around, talked about life, and had a few drinks. I was genuinely bonding with my pops. It was great, and I hoped we'd get to do it again sometime. We had already made plans to get together again. I knew something seemed strange when Duke and Carlos—some of Jorge's boys—came looking for me. How did they find my house? No one knew where I lived. I always made it a point to never let anyone take me home for that very reason, something I picked up from some friends of mine as a teenager. But I figured I better go on before I made Jorge any more upset. So, I hugged Pops and told him that I would be going out with some friends for the night. He told me he loved me and to try and stay out of trouble. That was the last night I would see him alive.

When we all got to Jorge's house, the boys ambushed me. Jorge told me he saw me with his girl again. I tried to deny it, but the sudden pain in my stomach from Jorge's fist kept me from saying anything. Jorge told me that enough was enough. I would have to pay for messing with his girl. And pay I did.

They broke in the house, tied my father up, and forced me to drag him to death in my car. My father didn't deserve that! I never spoke to Callie again; she tried to talk to me, but I told her to leave me alone. I didn't want anything to do with her or Jorge anymore. I didn't mean what I said about Callie, but I couldn't help it. Being with her was what made me lose my pops. Twenty-four years old with no friend left in the world. Mama gone, Daddy gone. I had nobody. But I guess Jorge had a point to make, and that he did. Pop's death hurt me bad, just like Jorge wanted it to. I couldn't take being without my pops or living with the conviction that I'm the reason he was gone. That's why the neighbors found me in the shed with a bullet through my head a few months later.

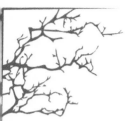

Callie Martinez

My name is Callie Martinez. I am the girlfriend of one of the most infamous men in Kentucky. However, my affections began to go to Jefferson around the time he died. His death showed me that this—Jorge—was my life, and always would be whether I wanted it to be or not.

I was born in Mexico in 1922 into a poor family. We didn't have nothing, and I mean nothing. Twelve children born to a father who made tools and a mother who worked as a nurse to help support us. They worked themselves down every day, but it wasn't enough. I, being the oldest child, wanted to help my parents and do something to help take the burden off.

So, I went into prostitution.

I made decent money that way. Most of the men in my town knew who I was so they stayed away from me, but when white men started coming to

Mexico, that's when the money started coming.

That's how I met Jorge.

Jorge was a mixed breed—a Mexican father and a black mother. Around that time in America, Mexicans were being brought back by the government to Mexico. The soldiers wanted just him and his mother to go, but his father refused to be separated, so the entire family was relocated.

He was of average height and build, wavy black hair, and had an average voice - not too high, not too low. Nothing very outstanding about him physically, but he had passion, which was something you didn't find in men very often. He also had money, which I, a poor girl at the age of 16, gravitated to instantly. That was just a part of the game.

When our relationship began, Jorge was shy and sweet. He would stop by the house and bring me gifts; it started out with jewelry and my favorite pastries and grew into things like clothes and cars. He would take me out to some of the most beautiful places in Mexico and let me rub elbows with some pretty powerful men who also become customers. I was his prime companion for several years. Of course, I would have to give my services in exchange, but I was getting the money and resources I needed to help my family, and that was all that mattered.

Eventually, Jorge let me know that things needed to change. I'll never forget that night. Jorge and I had just finished up one of our usual romps for the night and decided to take a moment to hang out in his car. That car was gorgeous. It wasn't the average kind of car you'd find in Mexico—it had to be from America. The car was yet another way Jorge separated himself from the pack and flexed his wealth.

I remember looking over at him and telling him how great of a time I had that night. I always had fun with Jorge. I went to turn away but I felt Jorge's hand lightly graze my chin. "Callie, I want you to be more than just a girl on my arm. I want you and only you, forever." This was all so new to me! No boy had ever said those words to me before! It was all so perfect! Maybe too perfect... but his eyes. His eyes were so sincere, I couldn't doubt him if I wanted to. Jorge and I became engaged in the Spring of 1933 and we moved to Kentucky where he claimed to have some business ties. It was this move that showed me who Jorge truly was. Kentucky was a different kind of place for me. Perhaps if we would have gone somewhere closer to home, the adjustment would have been easier on me, but Kentucky looked nothing like home. The blacks were nice, but the white people didn't like Mexicans, and it was hard at first because I spoke broken English. I spent the first year of my marriage depressed; the letters from my family back home were the only things that kept me going. Of course, Jorge tried to help, but he was so busy with his work that he didn't always have time for me. It was hard. I would talk to him about it but he would tell me to go out and try to make friends, just not male friends. I did try, but it was hard when I couldn't communicate. So, I taught myself English by listening to the local women gossip amongst each other.

As I was finally starting to learn English, I started seeing Jorge for who he really was. I didn't really understand all his conversations at first but as my English got better and better, I started to realize that Jorge was doing a lot of stuff, both in front of my face and behind my back. And it just got worse and worse. It would be normal for me to be shaken awake in the middle of the night by Jorge, telling me to go sleep on the couch because he brought someone home with him. As I would be fixing dinner for him and his friends, I started to understand that he would tell them how stupid and boring I was and how I had no clue about anything going on. Instead of eating what I cooked for breakfast, Jorge would lock himself in the bathroom and snort cocaine for hours on end. But I can say that one thing he never did was hit me, and he never deprived me of any material thing I wanted. He may have spit on me and jerked me around at times, but he never abused me the way he could have. Looking back on it, I think to myself, *How stupid was I?* I allowed myself to live like that for so long. I was being abused but continued to love Jorge and deny that the abuse was going on. But what could I have done? I was thousands of miles away with one Jorge to lean on. What could I really have done?

I first met Jefferson around 1942 at a cockfight that Jorge was hosting at our house. I had heard of Jefferson from conversations Jorge had. Jefferson was a dangerous man. It was rare to hear about him losing a bet and people knew he had to be worth a pretty penny. But Jefferson wasn't like other gamblers I had come to know. He wasn't like anyone I had ever met, actually. He was very down to earth and sweet—he was a breath of fresh air. And as I got to know him, I started to realize how bad Jorge was treating me. Jefferson and I would sit down for hours and talk about absolutely nothing, but those would were some of the best conversations I ever had. Books, food, music, life. Jefferson was smart and funny. He always knew how to raise my spirits. Of course he wasn't perfect, but he was just right for me. I still carry the conversations and wisdom Jefferson shared with me to this day.

Before his father was killed, Jefferson started treating me a bit funny. He wouldn't look at me and he would brush me off, which wasn't normal for him. I assumed that he was just going through something with his father and needed time, but after two weeks I couldn't take it anymore. I missed him too much. I took it upon myself to follow him one day and confront him about it, but he just told me to leave him alone, that we couldn't be friends anymore. I asked Jorge about it and he told me that Jefferson didn't need to be messed with. He was doing some shifty back-handed business that we didn't need any part of, and I had no business talking to him anyway. I didn't believe Jorge one bit, but what choice did I really have? A few nights later, Jorge was high again. He grabbed me by my shoulders, looked me in the eye with that odd grin of his, and told me that he had a job for me to do. He wanted me to take him to Jefferson's father's house and pretend that I was alone and lost so I could get into the house. After that, just wait. Those were all the instructions he gave me. I was too afraid to ask, so I just agreed. I did as I was told and approached Mr. Julius's house. I had been to the house before; Jefferson and I went for a ride one day and he showed me where his father's house was. Something inside me told me that this was going to end badly, but I didn't want anyone to hurt me so I knocked on the door.

Mr. Julius looked so kind—I knew his son had his eyes. We shared small talk and he was writing down directions for me. I kept peeking out of the window, wondering what was going to happen next. I didn't know. I was just afraid for my own life.

And then it happened. Jorge and the boys barged in through the door and grabbed Mr. Julius. He was so shocked, it looked as if he almost died right there.

I stayed in the house, afraid to do anything else, when suddenly I heard another car pull up. I went to look outside and saw Jefferson had pulled up with some of the other boys! I was so shocked and confused. Did Jefferson want his father dead? But then I looked closer; he was crying, and there was a gun at his head. I wanted to run out but I was scared. I didn't know what to do.

The next thing I heard was Jorge's voice yelling at Jefferson to drive. I knew Jorge was heartless, but this was something I had never seen before. Forcing someone to torture and murder their own father? I can only imagine how much pain and anguish Jefferson was feeling... I didn't see Jefferson again after that. The last I heard of him was that he had shot himself in his father's backyard. So sad. Life is hard, but sometimes things happen. I really liked Jefferson, but some things aren't meant to be. I've learned that. It's been the story of my life. He just couldn't play by the rules; he was too soft for the game and he had to learn how to play the hard way. I just wish he would have stuck around a little bit longer. We could have really been something, you know?

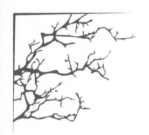

Jorge Algarin

I told him to leave her alone. He didn't listen. So, I had to... fix his hearing a little bit.

Callie was cute. She was a cute, little country girl that I instantly fell for when I met her in Mexico. Did I love her? Of course. But the longer we were together, the more I realized that it wasn't the kind of love she needed. Callie wanted me to love just her, a traditional type of love; I just couldn't do that. But I couldn't lose her either. She was a good woman, and I needed her on my side. The lifestyle I was in, a marriage wouldn't have worked out. That's why I never could marry her. But I did love her; my vices just took precedence over her.

Gambling was my lifeline. Women and drugs were my pastimes. I was good at it, I made money from it, and people respected me for it until Jefferson came around.

Jefferson was a great kid, just kind of lost. The guy had a great heart and a great spirit; he just used his heart too much when he should have used his head. That's what I couldn't stand about him. I could see his feelings for Callie early on. I wanted to deny it at first, but it was undeniable—it was obvious.

It made me furious. I tried to hide my jealousy too, but that gradually became harder and harder. I think Callie knew; she was nervous. But I saw in her a newfound sense of self and happiness. She was falling in love, and it wasn't with me. So, I did what I had to do.

I don't know why I felt like I had to do it. Maybe I loved her more than I thought I did. She hurt me, so I wanted to hurt her and him. I knew Jefferson's heart was his pops; I overheard him telling Callie that one day. The old man was the only family he had. That was the best way to hurt him and, with the way Callie was, I knew it'd break her too.

We set it up so that Callie would set the trap for Pops. I can still see the fear in her eyes when I told her to do it, or I'd kill her too. It gave me a rush. I got that same rush when we grabbed Pops and let his son do our dirty work. If anybody asked, we would tell them that Jefferson did it with his own car. We wouldn't be lying, right? Callie stayed. She didn't have a choice. It's not like she could go back to Mexico; she didn't have any money. She was mine until her very last breath. And that's exactly how I wanted it.

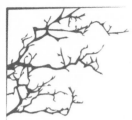

5
1952:
Shelly and Narvelle
Lavender

“ I'm Shelly and this is my twin sister Narvelle.”

"Hey," whispered Narvelle.

"Narvelle's real shy. I'm not, though. I love to talk. My mama used to say I'd talk Narvelle's ears off one day."

"Me and Shelly died."

"Yeah. They strangled Narvelle and I died of a head injury."

"Tell 'em, Shelly."

"You don't wanna tell it?" asked Shelly.

"No."

"Well, alright then. Well, some boys took us to a barn and raped us. I don't know why they chose us, but we were the ones they got. Folks thought we were crazy. Kids at school used to tease us and tell us that we were both crazy and that's why our parents were poor."

"April 19, 1952," Narvelle whispered shyly.

"Right, Narvelle. That's the day we died. We died together; we were twelve years old. Tell 'em what happened to you, Narvelle." "A big group of men... they touched me in private places and did bad stuff to me. Then they held a big thing around my neck and wouldn't let go."

"What Narvelle means is that the men raped her and strangled her.

Narvelle has down syndrome but I'm perfectly fine. I was hit in the head and died, though. We came into this world together, and that's exactly how we left it. But I'm getting too far ahead of myself. Let me start at the beginning.

"Narvelle and I were walking home from the store when Peter Timothy, Ralph Ingram, Tommy Lee Hornsby, and Mr. Shelton's son... uh, what's his name, Shelly?"

"Neal Avery."

"—and Neal Avery called us over. They said they had some extra candy that we could have. Tommy Lee used to sneak Narvelle candy all the time and she'd share it with me, so I thought it was gonna be okay. He always had the best candy. His uncle owned a candy store down the street from school. Black kids couldn't go in unless they had a white friend that would go in and buy stuff for them, so I was always happy when Tommy Lee would give us candy. But anyway, they called us over and as soon as we got in there, they grabbed us both up and carried us to opposite sides of the barn."

"They wouldn't let us go, Shelly."

"I know, Narvelle, I know," Shelly said as she grabbed her sister's hand.

"They took my clothes off and touched me in my private area. It hurt a lot and I wish they would have stopped. I screamed a lot."

"I know, Narvelle. It's okay, you don't have to talk about it."

"They called me stupid and ugly."

"It's alright, Narvelle," said Shelly. "They called us both dumb niggers. I could hear them raping my sister. They would hit her if she fought or cried too hard. I tried to fight the boys off of me and help Narvelle, but they hit me and knocked me out too. I hated we ever went in there.

As they attacked us, all I could think about was my mom and dad. I know they were worried about us, and I knew they were looking for us. And it made me sad, 'cause I knew they would probably never see us again."

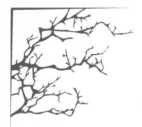

Peter Timothy

I don't know what we were thinking—we were just messing around. You know how boys are at that age. We were young, dumb, and curious. We wanted to know what it would be like to have an experience with a colored girl. We'd always heard colored girls felt different, so we wanted to try. We were only sixteen and seventeen at the time, and we knew we would be dead in the grave if anyone found out about it, so we just decided to try out those two Lavender girls. We knew they wouldn't say nothing 'cause everybody thought they were strange and they were both dumb. We also knew that no one had touched them yet. We thought we had the perfect plan put together.

We lured the dumb one with some candy, and her sister followed. Tommy Lee used to give them extra candy 'cause Shelly would always give him a kiss on the cheek after. He always had a thing for colored girls. So we knew she would follow if he called her. When we got them both in the barn, half of us took Shelly and the other half took Narvelle. The one sister who followed fought, so one of the boys hit her real good and knocked her out so they could have their way with her while we worked on Shelly.

It was something. They had never been touched before or nothing, and their skin was so soft. We wondered if this was what it was like with all black girls, but we had had our fix. We didn't want to get too carried away. If anyone found out about our curiosity, we'd have been dead for sure. Especially Tommy Lee, 'cause his dad was the sheriff.

We didn't think the dumb one would know what happened to her, but she started screaming at us and yelling for her sister and for help, and we panicked. We couldn't just leave her there, and it would look suspicious if we ran away with this screaming girl left behind to rat us out, so the same boy that knocked her sister out, knocked her out, but she was bleeding a lot. We panicked and decided to make it look like she had been lynched so folks would think it was the KKK. So that's what we did. We tied some rope we found around her neck and tied it real tight, so we'd make sure she couldn't breathe. At the same time, the other one woke up. When she saw her sister hanging, she started yelling and fighting, so one of the other boys began fighting back. He pushed her down and made her hit her head on the corner of a tractor. Her head immediately burst open, and she started bleeding out.

What did we do? We ran, of course! We didn't wanna get in trouble. Do you realize how embarrassing it would have been for the town to find out that we were playing with nigger girls? We wouldn't have ever been able to show our faces in school again!

Sometimes I sit and think about those girls. That was an experience I will never forget. White girls feel much different from them.

Sheriff Hornsby

I would be lying if I said it wasn't a gruesome scene. But people should know their place. If everybody did, none of these kinds of things would happen. Was this the first time I've seen something like this? No, not really. This was the first time I've seen two at one time, though. I was in my office when I got a phone call from the owner of the barn, Mr. Gentry. He found two dead colored girls in his barn. He said his son found them when he was going to get the tractor. I honestly wasn't too worried about it, but I know that kind of thing can interfere with his work so I went on down there to check it out. I tell you, it was pretty bad. The girls' clothes were torn off, blood was every which way you could imagine. One was slouched over on the wall with a great big gash on her head. The other one was just naked, hanging from the tree right next to the barn, her privates covered in blood. It was a rough sight to see.

We did try to investigate, but it wasn't much use. We didn't know much about the girls, other than their mama was a housekeeper and their daddy was a farmer out in the country. We let them know what happened and gave them the bodies. But we never did convict anybody of the murder. We had a few ideas, but we never had enough evidence to lock anyone up. A few nights after it happened, my wife told me that she overheard my boy and some of his friends talking about it. She claimed that they admitted to doing it and that Ralph and Timothy had scratches on their arms and faces from the struggle. But I told her it wasn't nothing to worry about. No evidence, no case. The boys liked to roughhouse a lot, so those scratches could have come from anywhere. All that was there was the colored gals' blood. Nothing else.

But really, come on, they were just two colored girls. Heck, one looked like she wasn't right anyway. May have been better off what happened. Their mama and daddy didn't have to be bothered. Two less mouths to feed.

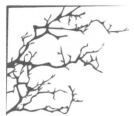

Littie Lavender

How would you feel if your daughters were kidnapped, raped, and murdered? And not just one, but two! Two! Both my babies are dead! DEAD! And it's just swept under the rug as if nothing ever happened or as if they deserved it! Can you believe that? Two little girls "deserved" to be raped and killed? No! I'll never accept that!

But the sad part is that there's nothing we can do about it. No justice will be served, no one will apologize, and my children will never get to rest in peace. I will never be able to rest in peace. My heart is beyond broken. And, as much as I hate to feel this way, I hope that those boys who did this to my babies are tortured with guilt until they repent and do what they are supposed to do. I truly do believe that you reap what you sow, and I know that God will take care of them. As hard as it is to wait, God will handle it.

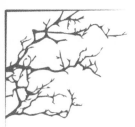

Neal Lavender

My daughters. My only two children in the world are gone and they aren't coming back. As a man, do you know how crushing that is to your soul? I'm supposed to be the man; I'm supposed to be able to keep my family safe... but I failed my daughters. I failed them.

Shelly and Narvelle needed me and I wasn't there for them! I failed my wife. There's nothing I can do now or ever in this lifetime to make this right or easy for Littie. We can't have no more children. It was a struggle for us to just have the girls, and now it's all gone! All wasted! I have an older son, but my wife has no children left. How am I supposed to make this better? All my wife ever wanted was children. She loved being a mother, and now our girls are gone!

When she wakes up in the middle of the night crying, what am I supposed to tell her? Am I supposed to tell her that it's gonna be okay? It's not gonna be okay! We'll never get to see them graduate from school, we'll never get to see them get married or have their own babies. My wife lost her only two children in the most terrible way possible! And not only that, but no one will ever be punished for it. It's never gonna be okay!

Since it happened, there's been some talk; I've been told about the boys who did this. They're known to lust over the young black ladies around town. I knew they were a dirty group of boys, but never in my life would I have expected them to do something as terrible and sick and evil as this. Especially not with my girls—my girls never bothered anybody. They didn't have many friends and didn't get into any trouble. They were too young to even be around those boys. What business do two twelve-year-old colored girls got with some sixteen and seventeen-year-old white boys? Explain that to me!

I don't care what happens to me, if I catch even one of them alone... only God knows what I'll do to them. And I have a couple of people who are ready and willing to help me with the others, too. I couldn't save my girls, and I hate myself every day for it. But I refuse to fail their memories and not make sure I watch the monsters who killed them suffer. That's the least I can do for Shelly and Narvelle.

I know the good Lord says that vengeance is His, Littie says it all the time, but I feel like I need to claim this one for myself. I can't let my family down again. I just can't...

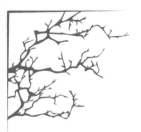

Epilogue

I f you are reading this, thank you.

Thank you for being courageous and enduring this journey.

Thank you so much for listening to the silenced speak their peace.

Now, a question to you: Think back on the individuals you have come to know along this journey. Does it change how you look at the concept of lynching? Did it bring an even more bitter taste of America into your mouth, or has it brought forth a new flavor you never knew existed?

Imagine if CJ or Malcus were still here. How could they have changed the world? Would Ruby have had her baby?

What kind of man would Garrett have been if he were able to have his mother in his life?

Would Jefferson and Callie have had a family? Could Jefferson's relationship with his father have improved?

How did Shelly and Narvelle's death impact their parents' marriage? Do you think the situation changed how Peter approached relationships and sex in his adult life? Did he feel any remorse? Did his friends attack other girls?

Sadly, the answers to these questions will never be. They can only be answered by our imaginations. The voices of these individuals were eternally silenced. Their history was denied. As a result, the people around them were forever changed.

These people were never given a chance to develop their gifts and talents and share them with the world. Some of them never had the chance to have families and bless the world with their legacies. Some of their families were so broken and afraid that no one was ever able to learn of their stories and experiences.

But the world will know now.

Their voices are no longer silenced. They are now able to rest in peace, their voices able to ring into eternity, forever vindicated.

Acknowledgements

First, I would like to give honor and praise to God. He was the one who gave me this gift and allowed me to finally achieve my goal of becoming a published author.

To my parents, thank you for loving me, supporting me, and encouraging me in my creative expressions and efforts, whether you understand them or not.

To my three big sisters, thank you for being my biggest cheerleaders throughout this process and my entire life. You guys are the best.

To my Aunt Gloria, thank you for being open to listening and celebrating with me in my success. You're the best aunt anyone could have.

To Linda Sullivan, thank you for always speaking into my life, even as a toddler. You always told me I'd be something great, and I thank you for being so supportive.

To the Pontotoc Writer's Group, you guys are amazing. Thank you for being open to my style and listening to my drafts as I polished this piece.

To my dear friends Thomas McRae and Clinton Williams, thank you for your patience, support, feedback, and friendship. You are awesome.

And lastly, I would like to thank the characters in the pages you just read. These were their stories, not mine. Thank you for allowing me to share your truths.

About the Author

Jessica Starks has a deep love for Southern Gothic writing, and always manages to find a way to sprinkle inspiration from the genre in her work. Writing a book was always on her bucket list, and eventually, with *The Lynching Calendar*, her dream became a reality. When not absorbed in her writing, Jessica loves reading, genealogy, watching old movies, and playing games with her family. She lives in Mississippi, surrounded by family and friends.